ISBN 1 85854 654 0
© Brimax Books Ltd 1998. All rights reserved.
Published by Brimax Books Ltd, Octopus Publishing Group Ltd.
2-4 Heron Quays, London E14 4JP, England
Reprinted 1999.
Printed in Spain.

SOMETIMES I AM NAUGHTY

by Gill Davies
Illustrated by Teri Gower

Brimax

Contents

Sometimes I am Naughty

I have a little sister
Who is as good as good can be.

Sometimes I am naughty
Though I do not mean to be.

My sister's very happy
She smiles all the time;

But sometimes I feel angry,
I scowl and stamp and whine.

My sister's toys are tidy
And sit neatly on the shelf.

Mine are scattered everywhere
In a mess, just like myself.

My sister's face is clean,
Her skin is scrubbed and shiny.

My face is streaked with paint
And my knees keep getting grimy.

When we are going out,
My sister's ready and on time.

But I am always late
And there's something I can't find.

My sister holds on tightly
When we walk the dog outside.

Why do I always drop the lead
So the dog runs off to hide?

When we draw a picture
Hers are always fine.

My crayon seems to wander off
And make a scribbly line.

My sister's very brave.
She says, "I like it in the night."

But I am frightened of the dark
So I need my own night-light.

I love my little sister
She's as nice as nice can be.

But sometimes I just wish
She was a little more like me!

Please Make Magic Real

It can happen in a fairy story
But I want magic to be real,

Not just something in a book...
I want to know how real magic feels.

I want to ride a magic carpet
And over mountains fly.

Or find a genie in a bottle
Or a beanstalk in the sky.

I want to have some magic
That happens and is true.

I want to have my wishes granted,
And meet an elf or two.

How I'd love to find a fairy
Hiding in a flower.

So her tiny wings stay dry
In a sudden summer shower.

It would be great to learn to fly myself
And go whizzing through the air;

Or find the rainbow's end
And the pot of gold that's there.

I would love to watch a wizard
Wave his wand…how I should stare

As wispy smoke, and stars,
And ghosts, rise up into the air.

It would be fun to make things disappear.
As fast as you could blink

And to talk to all the animals
And know exactly what they think.

I want my fairy godmother
To cast me a magic spell.

And how exciting if a frog prince
Lived in my wishing well.

But perhaps if real witches,
Or a giant, came to call

I should be glad that magic things
Are not really there at all!

I Want to Help

Everyone is busy today. Nobody will stop to play.

Mother is busy writing letters. I want to help, so I lick the stamps. Somehow they all stick to my tongue.

"Do go away and play quietly somewhere!" says Mother, sighing.

Father is busy mending the gate.

I want to help, so I jump on the gate to see if it will still swing back and forth.

"Go away!" says Father. "Go away now!"

I will go away and find my brother Martin.

Martin is busy too. He is making a toy plane. He says I am getting in the way.

I can't understand why he is so angry.

It wasn't my fault the glue spilt. And I did help him pick up all the pieces that somehow flew into the air when I breathed too close.

Grandpa is busy digging the garden.

I want to help. It is fun to pull up weeds and push them away in the wheelbarrow. But the wheelbarrow is too heavy for me. It rolls over Grandpa's foot and tips over.

"Those aren't weeds!" shouts Grandpa. "They are my new plants!"

I decide to go away and help Grandma instead. She is busy sewing a new dress for me.

I have forgotten the mud on my shoes and hands - and the glue on my fingers.

I can tell that Grandma does not really mean to be angry, but I go away anyway.

Mother is still busy writing the letters.

Father is still busy fixing the gate again.

Martin is still busy making another plane.

Grandpa is still busy replanting all his new plants.

Grandma is still busy. She is in the bathroom washing the mud and glue off my new dress.

I will just have to be busy on my own.

I write letters to all the toys.
"I want to help," says Teddy, but he delivers them to all the wrong toys.

I fix the gate on my toy farm.
"I want to help," says Teddy, but he somehow knocks the gate over.

I make some paper planes.
"I want to help," says Teddy, but he breathes too close and blows them away.

I put trees around the edge of my toy farm. Teddy pulls them up by mistake.

I cut out a paper dress for my doll. Teddy covers it with paw prints.

I am angry with Teddy - but I only shout a little bit because it is not his fault really. He just wants to help.

Then Mother comes in and says, "What a busy pair you and Teddy are – and nice and quiet too!"

She gives me a big hug. And I hug Teddy too.

If I were an Animal

I should like to be a rabbit.

His big ears can hear every sound, and his nose twitches as he stops to listen.

I burrow down to the bottom of my bed and pretend I am in a rabbit hole.

It would be fun to be a cat.

Cats have long tongues and can lick up every drop of milk. They purr when people stroke them.

I climb to the top of the highest tree and pretend I am a cat hiding in the leaves.

I wish I were a bird.

Birds can sing beautiful songs. They can fly high in the sky.

I jump off my bed and flap my arms and pretend to fly. I land with a bump and my brother laughs.

"Are you going to eat some worms now?" he laughs.

It would be nice to be a horse.

Horses have lovely, shiny coats and can jump over fences.

I find some string and make a mane and a tail to wear. Then I race around the house. Father says he cannot read his paper if I keep galloping and neighing.

It must be wonderful to be a pig. Pigs have a curly tail and are able to roll in the mud without their mother getting cross.

My brother laughs, "You don't need to pretend to be a pig."

I grunt back at him.

Being a frog would be fun.

Frogs can jump and swim and splash all day. No one is cross when they sit out in the grass in the pouring rain.

I pretend I am a frog in my bath. I croak and splash until the floor is wetter than a pond.

Bees have a good time. They can fly and hum and have lots of honey.

I climb into a box and pretend it is a hive. Then I fly out again and whiz in zooming circles around the room.

"Buzz off!" says my brother. So I pretend to sting him.

I think it would be best of all to be an octopus.

I could swim in the ocean and live in a cave. I would have lots of arms to hold all my toys. I could pick up far more cookies than my brother!

91

"If you were an octopus…" says Mother, tucking me into bed, "or a bird, or anything else at all, you wouldn't be my little boy. And I'd miss you a lot, you know."

I would miss Mother too, and Father and my nice warm bed, and Teddy. I might even miss my brother.

Perhaps it is best to keep being me!